BRAND
SPANKING
NEW!

Created by
Jim Jinkins

DOUG ™

COUNTS
DOWN

by Pam Muñoz Ryan

Illustrated by Matthew C. Peters • Tim Chi Ly • Alisa Klayman • Cheng-li Chan • Tony Curanaj • Brian Donnelly •
John Brandon

Disney
PRESS

NEW YORK

How did I get into this mess? It was Porkchop's birthday and I didn't have any money. So I went to ask Mr. Swirly if I could ride the Swirly Cycle and sell ice cream. That way, at the end of the day, I could buy Porkchop enough of his favorite treats for a BIG birthday celebration. And his favorite treat is Mr. Swirly's frozen Peanutty Buddy.

I met Mr. Swirly after school and explained that I needed to make some extra money.

"Sure, Doug," Mr. Swirly said, "you can help me today. Let's load the cycle. Uh-oh. I'm getting low on Peanutty Buddies."

I counted the Peanutty Buddy Cones in the Swirly Cycle. There were only TEN. I hoped there would be enough left at the end of the day for a big birthday celebration.

Our first stop was Beebe Bluff Middle School. Mr. White ran out of his office.

"As the principal of this school, I need to support the local businessman, especially if I want to run for mayor again someday!" said Mr. White. "I'd like one Peanutty Buddy, please."

I said, "Uh, Mr. White, I hear the Bobanna Nanna Bars are pretty tasty. Would you like to try one of those instead?"

"No, thank you, Dan, just a Peanutty Buddy Cone please."

That left NINE.

Mr. Fort, the band director, called to us from the football field where the band practiced.

He yelled, "Over here, Doug! I'll take a Peanutty Buddy Cone!"

"Mr. Fort, there's a special on Banana Bombs. How about one of those?"

"Absolutely not! Bananas are for babies," yelled Mr. Fort.

Now there were only EIGHT Peanutty Buddy Cones.

Skeeter was standing at the curb with his dad.

"What are you doing?" asked Skeeter.

"I'm working for Mr. Swirly so I can earn enough money to buy Porkchop a birthday present," I said.

"Cool, man," said Skeeter.

Mr. Valentine said, "I'll have one of those cold, creamy things, um, in a cone. The one that's got peanuts and, um, it's friendly . . ."

"A Peanutty Buddy Cone?" said Skeeter.

"Yeah, that's it," said Mr. Valentine.

"I'll have a Frozen Frothy Goat and my dad will have a Peanutty Buddy Cone," said Skeeter.

I didn't have the heart to try to convince Mr. Valentine to order something else. That left only SEVEN, but I wasn't worried . . . yet.

My sisters, Judy and Cleopatra Dirtbike, waited in front of my house.

"My brother is an ice-cream man," said Judy. "You must be kidding, Dougie."

"Who, me, kid?" I said. "I'm working so I can buy Porkchop a birthday present."

"How capitalistic," said Judy. "Hurry and give me a Peanutty Buddy Cone before my friends see you."

"Judy," I said, "I heard Peanutty Buddies give people a rash."

"Don't be dramatic, Dougie; that's *my* territory. I've had them before," she said.

I handed her the ice cream.

Only SIX left! Thank goodness Dirtbike was too young for ice cream.

Mr. Dink waved at us to come over.

"Douglas, an ice cream would be perfect right now. I have been clipping my hedges with my new Ice Creamcycle 2000 frozen-dessert–powered hedge trimmers. They're very powerful and very expensive. I'd like a Chocolate Swirly-Cue for myself, and I'd like one Peanutty Buddy for the trimmer. It's her favorite!" said Mr. Dink.

I gave Mr. Dink the Chocolate Swirly-Cue and the Peanutty Buddy Cone.

Oh, no! HALF of the Peanutty Buddy Cones were already gone! Only FIVE left!

Chalky jogged over to the Swirly Cycle.

"One Peanutty Buddy, please," he said. "I need a sugar rush before the big football game. We're undefeated, you know."

I groaned. "Chalky," I said, "how about a sugar-free high-energy carbo-bar instead?"

"Thanks, but no thanks, Doug," said Chalky. "I never change anything. It's unlucky before a big game."

I handed over the Peanutty Buddy.

"Good luck, Chalky," I said.

My hopes for a big birthday celebration were disappearing with each Peanutty Buddy Cone. Now I counted FOUR.

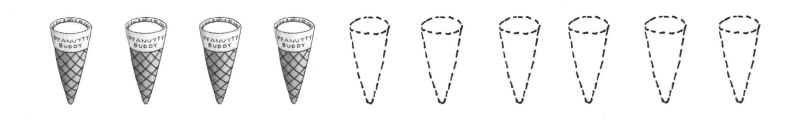

We stopped at Beebe's house. Beebe stood on the front steps of her mansion. She waved at us and sent Jinkins, her butler, down to the Swirly Cycle.

"One Peanutty Buddy Cone for Miss Bluff, and charge it, please!" said Jinkins.

One, two, THREE Peanutty Buddy Cones left! *Now* I was worried.

And so was Porkchop.

Next door, Roger waited with a wad of money.

"Hey, Funnie, nice hat!" said Roger.

I ignored him.

"Gimme a Peanutty Buddy Cone," said Roger.

"Um, they're not very fresh. How about a nice, juicy Frozen Blueberry Bing Bang?" I said.

Roger looked into the truck. "Hey! Don't try to con a con man. Hand over a Peanutty Buddy, pronto!"

As Roger turned away, I looked at what was left. Only TWO Peanutty Buddy Cones!

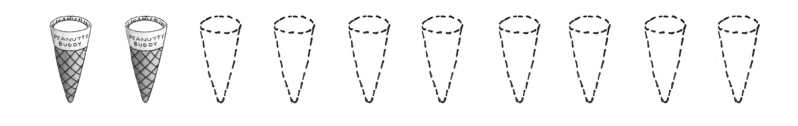

Then Roger turned back and yelled, "Hey, Funnie! I almost forgot. I need one more Peanutty Buddy Cone for my cat, Stinky."

"Roger, um, I heard ice cream is bad for cats. It makes them barf or something," I said.

"Funnie, I know what I'm doing," said Roger. "I'm smarter, remember? And I know what my Stinky likes—right, Stinky?"

"Rouwwwww!" said Stinky.

That left ONE lonely frozen Peanutty Buddy Cone in the Swirly Cycle.

Just then, Patti Mayonnaise waved to me from the basketball court.

"Hi, Doug," said Patti. "We're all worn out from playing basketball, and ice cream would taste great right now."

"One Grape Swirling Dervish," said Mr. Mayonnaise.

"I'd like a Peanutty Buddy Cone," said Patti.

I had to think fast.

"Well, we've, um, run out of a lot of flavors, Patti. How about a Berry Berry Frosty Doo, instead? I hear they're great!"

"Um . . . sounds tempting, but I'd really like a Peanutty Buddy. Do you have any left?"

I looked into Patti's eyes. My stomach did flip-flops. My heart pounded . . . and I handed over the last Peanutty Buddy Cone.

Then I realized what I had done. I had sold the last Peanutty Buddy Cone. There were none left. ZERO. ZILCH. Nothing for Porkchop.

All TEN were gone!

Porkchop whimpered.

I watched my best nonhuman friend in the whole world head toward home.

I had just ruined Porkchop's birthday celebration. I, Doug Funnie, felt like a failure.

I felt terrible. Even after Mr. Swirly paid me, I didn't have enough money for anything else on Porkchop's list. But on my way home, I had an idea. I stopped at Mr. Pooper's Party Paradise. The least I could do was buy some hats and party favors. Maybe they would make Porkchop feel better.

As I walked toward Porkchop's tepee, I practiced my speech. "Porkchop, I'm really sorry. I know you're the world's greatest dog . . ."

But then I heard music and laughter and what sounded like . . .

. . . a party!

Inside were all the people who had bought Peanutty Buddy Cones. And they had brought them to Porkchop for his birthday!

Well, what do you know, everything worked out just fine. We had a limbo contest and Porkchop won, of course. Mom and Dad even gave Porkchop a new remote control for his TV. I didn't get to buy Porkchop his favorite treat, but luckily everyone else did. And with the hats and favors, it turned out to be a really BIG birthday celebration after all!

Library of Congress Catalog Card Number: 97-67196
ISBN: 0-7868-3141-3

Original characters for "The Funnies" developed by Jim Jinkins and Joe Aaron.